J.J.E. Linton

Slavery in the Churches, Religious Societies & Co.

J.J.E. Linton

Slavery in the Churches, Religious Societies & Co.

Reprint of the original, first published in 1856.

1st Edition 2023 | ISBN: 978-3-37517-576-4

Salzwasser Verlag is an imprint of Outlook Verlagsgesellschaft mbH.

Verlag (Publisher): Outlook Verlag GmbH, Zeilweg 44, 60439 Frankfurt, Deutschland
Vertretungsberechtigt (Authorized to represent): E. Roepke, Zeilweg 44, 60439 Frankfurt, Deutschland
Druck (Print): Books on Demand GmbH, In de Tarpen 42, 22848 Norderstedt, Deutschland

SLAVERY

IN THE

CHURCHES, RELIGIOUS SOCIETIES, &c.

A REVIEW:

BY

THOMAS HENNING, Esq.,

WITH

PREFATORY REMARKS,

BY

J. J. E. LINTON, Esq.,

STRATFORD.

TORONTO:

PRINTED AT THE GLOBE BOOK AND JOB OFFICE, 22, KING STREET WEST.

1856.

PREFATORY REMARKS.

The following Review appeared in the "Globe" newspaper of Toronto, in November last (1855.) It was written by Thomas Henning, Esq., Secretary of the Anti-Slavery Society of Canada, at Toronto. It has no special relation to the "Report," which forms its title, beyond a passing reference to it. It goes over the subject generally, as applicable to the American churches in their support of and connection with Slavery. It occurred to the writer of these remarks, that the subject being so ably handled by Mr. Henning, it would be well to rescue by republication, such an important review on slavery, from the dormant files of a daily journal which, as is customary with newspaper periodicals, are laid aside after perusal, and get beyond the reach of reference. Such is the reason for its re-appearance and availing himself of the opportunity, these remarks are prepared.

We indite these prefatory remarks, under a depressing sense, as a man, that men, professed Christian men, admitted members of churches, permitted to take in their hands, at the communion table, the symbols of a crucified Saviour ; nay, that ministers of religion by their silence, by their expressed words, and by their ownership of slaves, are guilty of not only holding their fellow men in bondage as slaves, but committing directly or tacitly the gross outrages on these slaves, which no pen can adequately describe, or tongue, however eloquent, discourse upon. "Nothing of tragedy "can be written, can be spoken, can be conceived, that equals the frightful "reality of scenes daily and hourly acting in the United States, beneath the "shadow of American law and the shadow of the cross of Christ,"—truly, too truly, has Mrs. H. B. Stowe written.

We have no hesitation,—we consider it a duty, in stating, that if there is one thing more and above another, which will cause Infidelity, Deism, Freethinking, skepticism, and unbelief, as to the reception of Christianity, it is the present attitude in America, of certain Christian churches and societies, and of those who recognise and fraternise with them, in regard to the sin and evil of "AMERICAN SLAVERY." And in this statement, we are sorry to include the lukewarmness, apathy, frigidity, with a connection and a fellowship, of some of our Canadian churches and societies. If a prominency of intercession for the African race, is to be effected by Canadian churches, if a successful and benignant mission to non-Christian lands (*we* should hesitate to call them heathen lands !) is to be forwarded, it cannot be done by them Christianly, in their recognizing the American Tract Society, the American Sunday School Union, the Methodist Episcopal Church Book Concern, of 200 Mulberry Street, New York, the Presbyterian Board of Publication, 225 Chestnut Street, Philadelphia ; or any religious society or organization which has not, in open front of its constitution, the words, "We have no fellowship with American Slavery, and receive not its gains."

Let not the (Free) Presbyterian sh[illegible] from our allusion to the Presbyterian Board of Philadelphia, for though that Board publishes pure copies of books from the original, when they republish, (there is an exception, however,) which the American Tract Society does not do in all cases,* the Board is a part of the noted Pro-slavery General Assembly of the Presbyterian church of the U. S. (old school.) That Assembly has under its management at Philadelphia, the following Boards :—1. Publication, 2. Domestic Missions, 3. Education, 4. Foreign Missions,—the latter at New York, Revs. Dr. Lowrie and Mr. J. L. Wilson, Secretaries. And yet the Presbyterian Church (Free) of Canada, will " dilly-dally " and shake hands with that body openly, encourage their colporteurs in Canada, buy books &c., from them, colportage them in rural districts, and in every way act with that Board, as though the latter was not of a Pro-slavery church ! Away with the excuse which has been, and will again be made, that their copies of books are *pure* copies ! So is the golden eagle, silver coin, or bank note, of the Presbyterian Slaveholder, when paid in as a subcription, a contribution, or at a collection for that Church ! Such is not counterfeit money. Surely the divines in the Presbyterian Church in Canada, are not of to-day's teaching, as not to know, that the collections made and contributions received, a few years ago from slave-holders, by certain ministers of the Free Church of Scotland, who made a tour in the slave States, when paid in to the Treasury of the Free Church of Scotland were marked as the *price of blood;* and within a few yards of where we pen these words, in Stratford, there lives a Presbyterian, who on a visit to Scotland, was wit-

---

* So little is known to what extent the American Tract Society has been guilty, that independent of D'Aubigne's history, and several other books referred to by name, it may not be generally known that the celebrated book "Mammon," by Harris, and the cheering " Morning Exercises," by the late Rev. W. Jay, have been meddled with. See advertisement of 17th March, 1856, in Canadian papers.

ness to the cry of opposition, by the people, and saw the marked expression, the very buildings being well marked in many places in chalk writing, "give back the money, it is the price of blood !" Reference is most vividly made to the events at the time (1846–47) in the book, "My Bondage and My Freedom," by F. Douglass, p. 382. Mr. Douglass was then in Britain. The cry of opposition by the Presbyterian people of Scotland is not yet hushed. And with such and other prominent marks of a Christian disposition with the lay Presbyterians, shall the ministers of that Church dare to mock their people with an exhibition of any kind of contamination with a pro-slavery church or organization such as above alluded to ?

We have referred elsewhere (" *Colonist* " of 12th January,) to the standing of the Wesleyan Methodist Church in Canada, in its connection and fellowship with the pro-slavery Methodist Episcopal church (north) in the U. S. and adduced sufficient proof to sustain our accusation, notwithstanding' there was a *denial* of the same. " The Canada Sunday School Advocate,' having the addition of the word " Canada," being a reprint of the S. School Advocate, published at 200 Mulberry street, New York, continues to be published, *as if at Toronto*, by the Wesleyan Methodist Church in Canada, and there does not appear any symptoms of separation, or of a *protest* by the Canadian Church, against the evils of slavery countenanced in the W. M. Church (north.) But in the latter church, there may be another secession, or perhaps a division, on the slavery question, ere long—so thinks, the Pittsburg *Christian Advocate* and there has been a recent cause too in obtaining the services a few weeks since, of a slaveholding Bishop of the M. E. Church (south) from a plain pro-slavery church, to officiate at the dedication of a church at Newark, New Jersey (*Religious Telescope*, Dayton, Ohio.) The Wesleyan Methodist people in Canada, are kept in ignorance of these things, yet it is with such, their church in Canada, has a fellowship and connection. But this has been of long standing as the records of their church will shew. When will that fellowship and countenance have an end ?

The Methodist New Connection Church in Canada, has no such fellowship. We wish we could say as much of the Regular Baptists of Canada,—and we desire not to discourse further with the Congregational church,—yet there are exceptions of a "fellowshipping tendency" with some of its ministers also. We have never alluded to the Unitarian ministry; yet we cannot refrain at this time, in referring the " fellowshipping' churches above named, to the truly Christian, benevolent, and philanthropic resolutions passed at a meeting of that Body, held at Montreal, October, 1854, where about 300 ministers were present. They are worthy of being copied and acted upon, and will be found in the " Globe" (Toronto,) of 23rd October, same year.

That a *reform* is needed and required in the Christian church, no stronger evidence need be looked for, than that contained in the History of the chattel slavery of human beings, of the chattelizing system, whereby human beings are, by laws made by Christian men, held in bondage as a *thing*, the same as we hold or possess our horses, cattle, chairs, tables, musical instruments, books, and all chattel property ; and as liable to be privately or publicly sold, even to the separation of man, wife, and child,—even to the sale of a part of a man, or part of a woman. and of the babe itself while in the mother's womb, or at its birth ;—with the well authenticated instances of a parent selling his own sons and daughters, and of a brother selling his brothers and sisters !

That an Alliance,—a purely Evangelical Alliance,—is required to reform and Christianize the Christian Church, no honest historian, or a peruser of history and of things as they are, can for a moment hesitate to believe And one of the strongest grounds now existing, for such an Alliance, is that of human chattel slavery as recognised, countenanced, and participated in by————Christian divines and by Christian laymen.

We do not here allude to those portions of the world, called heathen, barbarian, or uncivilized, or to a "non-christian" people or country ; no, we simply confine our remarks to Christianized portions of our globe.

The Christian country, where such an Alliance might be more eminently formed, appears to be in the land of our birth, Great Britain. And there in London. Bristol and Leeds, in Edinburgh and Glasgow, exist associations, which have laudably laboured so far, by the promulgation of facts exhortations and incitements, for the entire reduction and abolishment of the vile system of chattel slavery.

In America (apart from the British Provinces) similar associations as the above, but not on such a free, and freeman's soil, will be found in Boston (Mass :) in New York city, also at Cincinnati, and at Dayton (Ohio). To be more exact, and for information to the enquiring mind, we refer to 48, Beekman Street, New York.

What is human slavery and its origin, and continuance, amongst Christians ? Reader, thinking man or woman, obtain and refer to the following books, and desire not to allege ignorance on the subject. These books can be obtained at any book store, or be ordered for you, and at a comparatively small price. Get any one of them : They are :—

1. The History of the Rise, Progress and Accomplishment of the Abolition of the African Slave Trade by the British Parliament, by the late

Thomas Clarkson, M. A. (originally published in 1808—Referable to it, the evidence taken before the House of Commons, is published by the American Reform Tract Society at Cincinnati, price 25 cents.)

2. A brief notice of American Slavery and the Abolition movement, By the late J. B. Estlin, F. R. C. S. Bristol (Eng :) 2d Edition, reprinted by the Leeds Anti-slavery Association (Eng :) 1853—Tweedie, 337 Strand London, pp. 54, (an excellent epitome on the subject.)

3. Key to " Uncle Tom's Cabin"—by Mrs. H. B. Stowe, Boston, 1854. This is an unanswerable book of facts and arguments.

4. Inside view of Slavery : By C. G. Parsons, M. D., Boston 1855, pp. 318. A book of facts.

5. The American Slave Code, by Rev. William Goodell, 3d. Edit., 1853, pp. 439. (Here will be found the *legal* relations with facts. A valuable book, with an excellent letter from Hon. W. Jay, prefixed.)

6. Slavery and Anti-slavery, by Do., 3d. Edit. 1855, pp. 606, (a complete review and history of slavery and anti-slavery movements, and especially slavery in connection with the American churches and societies.)

7. My Bondage and my Freedom, By Frederick Douglass, 1855, pp. 464. (Mr. Douglass is proprietor and editor of a newspaper called after his own name, at Rochester, N. Y.)

8. The Slavery Question, By Rev. John Lawrence, Dayton (Ohio), 3d Edit. 1854, pp. 224, (This book is the *multum in parvo*, on the subject, embracing all that is needed ; origin of slavery, its definition and illustration, slavery and religion, American churches and slavery, &c. This is a book which no man should be without, and states all that may be desired to be known. Get it.)

9. Letters on Slavery, addressed to the Pro-slavery men of America, showing its illegality in all Ages and Nations—By O. S. Freeman, pp. 108, Boston, B. Marsh, 1855. (This is a book filled with authorities. The Boston *Traveller* says, " these letters on slavery will form, for future use, an irrefutable text-book upon the subject.")

Many books and pamphlets &c., on the subject of slavery, can be obtained at the Abolition Depository, 48 Beekman Street, N. York, whose catalogues with prices, are issued. We briefly refer to " An Enquiry into the Scriptural views of Slavery,"—By Rev. Albert Barnes, Phil. 1855 : a perusal of this book would enlighten some pro-slavery minds. See review in " Independent," N. Y., 27th March, 1856.

If the present system of American Slavery, is much longer recognised and not more generally, openly and freely protested against, by Christian men, the Christian religion may soon only have an existence by name, in the United States of America !

The upholding of our common Christianity, our life and our hope here and hereafter, is, without doubt, much impugned and injured by the actions and opinions of pro-slavery men, of ministers, churches and religious societies. The beauty, the life, the warmth, the love, and the anchor of hope, of Christianity, all are being defaced and degraded, by sinful and brutal men, in the espousing, by the support, of American Slavery. The time has arrived when the character of a man, as man, may be judged of between men, in this wise : In the ordinary transactions of life, when information may be desired, the question will be "was such done or accomplished or achieved or supported by a *man*, or by a *Christian*"! And the opinion may follow also, in this wise : "No *man* will do that, no *Christian* should" ! Are we writing thoughtlessly or unjustly ? We hope not.

We have no hesitation then, in asserting, that no man *is* a man, and no Christian *is* a Christian (with the light of knowledge and of facts in this age revealed) who supports or coquets with, the system of American Slavery. But more than this, and we appeal for its truth to the philanthropist, the patriot, and the politician, the social truth is, that a basis of our own freedom, of all human freedom, consists in the proclamation " THAT AMERICAN SLAVERY IS A WRONG, IS A SIN, IS A CURSE."

We pray, however, that we may be spared to see the churches in the United States and in Canada, take that stand against any oppression of the human race by slavery, which as professed Christian churches they ought to take. Nurtured as our Canadian churches are, in world's goods, (however great or small) and with the prayers and good wishes of a loyal and a monarchical people, who claim as their prerogative to belong to an empire "on whose realms the sun does not set", and "whose flag has braved a thousand years, the battle and the breeze",—and who acknowledge, as an inscription on their temples of worship to a Supreme Jehovah, and on their edifices to Science and Art "that Britons never shall be slaves," and who declare an unfaltering and loving loyalty to our Gracious Queen VICTORIA, let all unite in repudiating every shade and plan of fellowship and connection, with pro slavery churches and societies.

STRATFORD, C.W., April, 1856.

J. J. E. LINTON.

SLAVERY IN THE CHURCHES, &c.

REVIEW.

REPORT OF THE NEW YORK GENERAL ASSOCIATION, (Congregationalist,) 26th August, 1855. With introduction by J. J. E. LINTON Esq. Stratford, C. W.

Amidst the numerous subjects that demand the attention of the public and challenge discussion, there always tower aloft above the rest, some, which, both on their own account, and because of the relations they bear to others, claim our special notice and call for earnest and unremitting action. Prominent amongst such subjects, stands at the present day, the question of human slavery, which is the source of so many and so great evils, social, political, economical. That man persists in keeping his fellow man in such an abnormal condition as slavery implies, is one of the strongest evidences of the degraded state into which our race has lapsed. That any man regarding slavery in the light of history and perceiving its ruinous effects in the case of individuals and of nations, can, notwithstanding such perception, palliate its enormities and advocate its perpetuation is unreasonable ; but in the case of a minister of the Gospel, a student of the Word of God, such conduct is truly monstrous. It is strange indeed, how any man, living under a Republican Government, which, in theory at least, maintains the right of the individual to life, liberty, and the pursuit of happiness, can, without feelings of detestation, witness the enthralment of three millions of his fellow men, without putting forth one effort for their enfranchisement ; but unsurpassably strange it is, how any one calling himself a teacher of that Gospel whose mission it is to " bind up the broken-hearted, to proclaim liberty to the captives, and the opening of the prison doors to them that are bound," to instruct the ignorant, to elevate the debased, can so prostitute his office as to tolerate a system which abrogates the family relation, encourages unchastity, violates the commonest instincts of human nature, and transforms those whom Christianity would make freemen of the Lord into the chattels of oppressive men. And yet, strange, monstrous as such a thing is, it is, alas, an every day occurrence. It is not mere worldly men—those who are living by the unrequited toil of their bondsmen—those who enrich themselves by trafficking in the bodies and souls of their fellow men— who act thus, but men who are called religious. American churches and ecclesiastical organizations of almost every denomination, utter but faint, if any, remonstrances against such practices; the ablest defences of slaveholding and of the return of the fugitive, have been written by leading clergymen, without forfeiture of ministerial standing; nay, they have thereby gained the highest honors and proudest positions in their respective bodies, whilst others, with at least equal talents, for bearing testimony against slavery, have been deserted, defamed and left without support. The leading religious periodicals, are either silent or are ranged on the side of the oppressor. The great Missionary organizations are timid and recreant, while Tract Societies, mutilate and corrupt the works they print, in order to save the conscience of the guilty slave-owner, and enrich themselves at the expense of truth and honesty, and every principle of upright dealing. In view of such facts, we are called upon, as members of the same family, to lift up the voice of warning and of expostulation. The cause of humanity and philanthropy knows no territorial limit, is bounded by no geographical lines. If a heathen could say that he regarded nothing that pertained to humanity to be foreign to him, much more are we bound by every consideration, to interest ourselves in the fate of those of our fellow men who, at our very doors, are treated as chattels personal, stripped of every attribute of humanity, and subjected under a Republican Government, through the action of their fellows, to cruelty more severe than despotism ever devised in any age.

' We had occasion lately to notice, though briefly, the proceedings of some of the religious bodies at their anniversary meetings in the United States and promised then to describe more fully, at a future time, the relation of these bodies to the great question of slavery. The publication of the tract whose title stands above, as well as some similar works which are now before us, affords us an opportunity of reviewing the subject in some of its numerous bearings, and of exhibiting the delinquencies of the Church in respect to this sin, which, without its countenance and encouragement, as the distinguished Barnes has honestly confessed, could not exist for a day.

In the first place it is worthy of remark, that the course of the Church in regard to the sin of slavery in the United States, has been for many years, as in the case of the State, a downward course. Goodell in his work entitled, " Slavery and Antislavery" shows us that the Friends in their yearly meetings took strong ground on the subject as early as 1776, enacting that "the owners of slaves, who refused to execute proper instruments for giving slaves their freedom, were to be excluded from membership or disowned." The Congregationalists also, in New England, were equally uncompromising, and about the same time, they resolved as a body, " that the slave trade and the slavery of the Africans, as it has existed among us, is a gross violation of the righteousness and benevolence which are so much inculcated in the Gospel, *and therefore we will not tolerate it in the Church*." Coming down a few years later [1780] we find the Methodist Societies using the following language : " The Conference acknowledges that Slavery is contrary to the laws of God, man and nature, hurtful to society, contrary to the dictates of conscience and pure religion, and doing what we would not that others should do unto us, and they pass their disapprobation upon all our friends who keep slaves, and they advise their freedom." Indeed we learn from Lee's History of the Methodists, page 101, that the Methodist Episcopal Church was organized with a number of express rules on the subject which stipulated THAT SLAVERY SHOULD NOT BE CONTINUED IN THE CHURCH ; and Wesley's tract on slavery, in which it was designated, as " the sum of all villainies" was distributed by the Methodist itinerant preachers as a part of their official business. The General Assembly of the Presbyterian Church adopted in 1794, a note to the 142nd question in the larger Catechism, in which they say, " The term *mansstealer*, in its original import, comprehends all who are concerned in bringing any of the human race into slavery or *retaining them in it*. Stealers of men are those who bring off slaves or freemen and KEEP, SELL, or BUY THEM." Further, Semple in his History of the Baptists in Virginia, says, that at a meeting of the General Committee in 1789, the Baptists resolved "that slavery is a violent deprivation of the rights of nature and inconsistent with republican government, and therefore we recommend it to our brethren to make use of every measure to extirpate this horrid evil from the land." Such was the position of some of the leading sects in regard to this question at that early day. Let us glance briefly at their course since that time, and at their present position. In 1801 the General Conference of the Methodist Episcopal Church said : " We are more than ever convinced of the great evil of African Slavery, which still exists in the United States." Observe here the studied dilution of the testimony of 1780, when slavery was admitted to be not merely " an evil " but a *sin*, contrary to the laws of God, man and nature." Coming down to 1836, we find the Conference held at Cincinnati, declare that they wholly disclaim any right, wish or intention to interfere with the civil and political relation of master and slave as it exists in the slave holding States of this union." This was adopted by a vote of 120 to 14. Why so great a change ? The answer is to be found in the fact that too many of the ministers were themselves slaveholders. In strict accordance with this resolution were the sentiments of the leading individual ministers of this church. For example, Prof. Simons of Virginia Conference declared, " that slavery which exists in America, was founded in right." President Thornton says that " God not only permitted Slavery, but absolutely provided for its perpetuation ; the act of holding a slave, then, is not a sin." Bishop Hedding, a Northern man, presiding at the New England Conference in 1838, refused to put resolutions condemning the buying and selling of slaves, and declaring slavery to be a moral evil. It has been asserted that since the division of the church in 1844, on the expediency of having slaveholding Bishops, the northern branch was anti-slavery. To this a sufficient answer will be found in the following statement lately made by *Zion's Herald*, a leading Methodist paper published in Boston. "Our church (north)" says the *Herald*, "tolerates slaveholding *ad libitum* in its LAITY ; a man owning a thousand slaves finds admission to her communion just as freely as a man who owns none. In a word, slaveholding works no more disqualification for membership in the Methodist Episcopal Church than it does in the Methodist Episcopal Church South." To corroborate this statement, the editor quotes a resolution of the Baltimore Conference, determining to keep travelling preachers free from Slavery but determining at the same time "not to *hold connection* with an Ecclesiastical body that shall make *non-slaveholding a condition of membership* in the church." In 1852, a prominent member of conference said : "Slaveholders claimed to be in the church by *right* and under the discipline of the church, and not merely by sufferance and tolerance ; and he (Mr. Collins) endorsed their views fully, and completely."

Turning now to the Presbyterian church we find a state of things precisely similar. In 1816 the General Assembly, while it called slavery a "mournful evil" directed the erasure of the note (of 1794) to the eighth commandment. In 1835, Mr. Stewart of Illinois a ruling Elder, in advocating sundry anti-slavery memorials, urged the General Assembly to take action on the subject. He said :

"In this Church, a man may take a free born child, force it away from its parents, to whom God gave it in charge, ' saying bring it up for me,' and sell it as a beast, or hold it in perpetual bondage, and not only escape corporal punishment, but really be esteemed an excellent Christian. Nay, even ministers of the Gospel and Doctors of Divinity may engage in this unholy traffic and yet sustain their high and holy calling. Elders, Ministers and Doctors of Divinity are, with both hands, engaged in the practice."

The facts were not disputed, a Committee was appointed which reported in 1836 that " the subject of slavery is inseparably connected with the laws of many of the States, with which it is by *no means proper for an Ecclesiastical body to interfere,"* and that "any action on the part of the assembly would tend to distract and to divide our Churches;" The matter was therefore indefinitely postponed. In 1838 the Church was divided into the Old and New Schools, but, differing on many points, there has been wonderful harmony on the subject of Slavery. From year to year the Old School body resolve "that it is of the greatest consequence to the best interests of the Church that the subject of Slavery shall not be discussed"; and there the question remains. The conduct of the New School on this subject has been vacillating and inconsistent in the extreme. At one time resolutions have been passed declaring Slavery unrighteous and oppressive, and exhorting to its abolition, but these are followed by others palliating and qualifying so as to neutralize all that preceded. Indeed no one can examine the action of the Church as a whole without concluding, with Mr. Goodell, that but little moral difference exists between the divided branches. "The one has more slaveholders under its jurisdiction than the other, but both tolerate the practice. The one does this to retain many members, the other to retain a few. The one does it believing Slavery to be a Bible Institution; the other, believing it to be ' unrighteous' and 'oppressive.' The one makes no pretence of any intention to discipline any sort of slaveholders, the other holds the rod over a class of them that it ' has no information' of being found within its enclosures, but yearns to go out of its boundaries to clasp them to its bosom."

The Congregationalists, the descendants and successors of the Puritans, of whom better might have been expected, have in their Associations and Consociations pursued a course practically the same. They have fraternized with slaveholding Presbyterians, have palliated by resolution and otherwise what they were forced to proscribe as sinful, and have condemned "slavery" rather than " slaveholding," a distinction not very perceptible to persons of ordinary intelligence. Prof. Stuart of Andover, by whom a large portion of the Congregationalist Ministers have been educated, and to whom they have been in the habit of looking up for instruction in scriptural truths, taught that the

existence of slavery was not sin; that the *abuse* of it was the
only essential and fundamental wrong; and therefore the
relation of master and slave may exist, *salva fide, et salva
ecclesia,* "without violating the Christian faith, or the
Church." And after the passage of the infamous Fugitive
Slave Bill in 1850, the Professor was amongst the first to
appear as the defender and eulogist of Hon. Daniel Webster,
for the part he took in procuring and advocating that iniquitous measure, and vindicated his defence at length in a
published pamphlet. Then again the publications of the
Congregational Body, such as the *Christian Spectator,* teach
that the Bible " contains no explicit prohibition of Slavery.
It recognises both in the Old and New Testaments, such a
constitution of society, and it lends its authority to enforce
the mutual obligations resulting from that constitution."
The Editor of the *Vermont Chronicle,* (Rev. Joseph Tracy)
now of the New York *Observer,* wrote of slaves, " that they
have no right to be taught to read *immediately.*" And
while advocating the education of such, " *would pass no
sentence either of condemnation or approval, on those who
withheld this art from their slaves.*"

The Baptists are not behind their brethren of other ecclesiastical organizations, in defending slavery and frowning
down all attempts at abolition. Southern Baptists teach
that " *adopting slavery as one of the allowed relations of Society,* Christ made it the province of his religion only to
prescribe the *reciprocal duties of the relation.* The Sa-
vannah River Baptist Association of Ministers decided in
1835 that the divine institution of marriage must be
modified in conformity with the slave code, and that slave
cohabitation, for the increase of their human chattels, may
be enforced by Ministers, without subjecting them to "*church
censure.*" In 1833, the Rev. Dr. Freeman, in an exposition
of the *views of Baptists,* said : " the right of holding slaves
is clearly established in the Holy Scriptures, both by pre-
cept and example." At the north there is delightful unity
with the south on this subject. The Rev. Dr. Bolles, of
Massachusetts, said, in 1834, " there is a pleasing union
among the multiplying thousands of Baptists throughout the
land ; our southern brethren are generally, both ministers
and people, slaveholders." " The great majority of north-

ern Baptists," says Mr. Goodell, endorse this statement and certify the essential identity of their religion with that of southern Baptists, by joining with them in sending THEIR religion *to the Heathen.*"

The position of the Protestant Episcopal Church may be learned from the testimony of John Jay, Esq., himself an Episcopalian, but a distinguished friend of freedom and of the slave. In a pamphlet entitled " Thoughts on the duty of the Episcopal Church, in relation to Slavery " he says—

" Alas for the expectation that she would conform to the spirit of her ancient mother! She has not only remained a mute and careless spectator of this great conflict of truth and justice with hypocrisy and cruelty, but her very priests and deacons may be seen ministering at the altar of slavery, offering their talents and influence at the unholy shrine, and openly repeating the awful blasphemy, that the precepts of our Saviour sanction the system of American Slavery. Her Northern (free state) clergy, with rare exceptions, whatever they may feel on the subject, rebuke it neither in public nor in private, and her periodicals, far from advancing the progress of abolition, at times oppose our Societies, impliedly defending slavery, as not incompatible with Christianity, and occasionally withholding information useful to the cause of freedom. Two sermons, justifying Slavery, preached by a clergyman in presence of Bishop Ives, (a native of a free state) were actually republished, as a religious tract, and the author was afterwards made Bishop of Texas !"

Such is the position of the leading religious sects in the United States on the subject of. Slavery. In the most of them there are noble exceptions as regards individual Churches, and in all of them, of members, who are most devoted friends of the slave ; but we are now writing of the general characteristics of the great body of the ministers and people. Regarding the smaller organizations, but little of a very satisfactory nature can be said. The Protestant Methodist Church (without Bishops) allows Slaveholding. The Dutch Reformed Church co-operates with Slaveholding Churches in Missionary enterprizes, though at the late general synod which met at New York, they refused to admit into fellowship the North Carolina classes of the German Reformed Church, some of whose ministers were Slaveholders. Unitarians, Universalists and Restorationists are divided on the Slavery question as all the others. The Freewill Baptists and the Scotch Covenanters take anti-slavery ground. The Cumberland Presbyterians refuse to legislate on the subject of slavery on the plea that " as spiritual bodies, they have no cognizance of civil matters." The Disciples, or Campbellites, are slaveholders and slaves—Campbell himself held that " there is but one verse in the Bible inhibiting it," and concluded that "it is not immoral." But the low views of the Church in regard to this whole question will be still more apparent when we come to consider the action of ecclesiastical Boards and Missionary Societies, a branch of our subject which we must reserve for a second article.

In reviewing the foregoing statements, then, as regards the Southern Church, we find the following principles established by them as summed up briefly by Mrs. Stowe in her Key to Uncle Tom's Cabin. For each of these statements we have documentary evidence before us. 1. That slavery is an innocent and lawful relation as much as that of parent and child, husband and wife or any other lawful relation of society. 2. That it is consistent with the most fraternal regard for the good of the slave. 3. That masters ought not to be disciplined for selling slaves without their consent. 4. That the right to buy, sell and hold men for purposes of gain was given by express permission of God. 5. That the laws which forbid the education of the slave are right, and meet the approbation of the reflecting part of the Christian community. 6. That the fact of slavery is not a question of morals at all, but is purely one of political economy. 7. The right of masters to dispose of the time of their slaves has been distinctly recognized by the Creator of all things. 8. That Slavery as it exists in the United States, is not a moral evil. 9. That without a new revelation from heaven, no man is entitled to pronounce Slavery wrong. 10. That the separation of slaves by sale should be regarded as separation by death, and the parties allowed to marry again. 11. That the testimony of colored members of the Churches shall not be taken against a white person. 12. That it is right and proper to put down all enquiry upon this subject by Lynch law.   What now is the position of the Northern Church ? One of deep complicity. All their influence, and it is mighty, has been thrown on the side of the oppressor. Their course has been one of temporizing and concession, until the distinction between North and South, in too many instances, has been obliterated. The friends of freedom and of the slave have been characterized as fanatics ; and men whose whole lives have been spent in acts of benevolence and mercy, have been shunned as infidels. The position of the various Northern Missionary Organizations will be gathered from the Tract which has been republished by Mr. Linton, and which he is distributing widely at his own expense. It is well worthy the attention of religious men, and especially, that portion of them on whom our Bible, Tract, and Sabbath School Societies depend for support.

SECOND ARTICLE.

In our previous article on the above subject, we traced briefly the course of the American Churches of all the leading denominations, and proved, we think, very satisfactorily, that that course has been one, not of progress, but of retrogression. We showed that, while almost every sect at one time or another spoke out plainly against slavery, and in most instances declared slaveholding *sinful*, all the great sects are at the present moment substantially harmonious in repudiating their quondam statements, and in declaring the institution of human slavery, as it exists in the United States, not necessarily sinful—in other words, not a sin *per se*. We adduced documentary evidence to testify that this is true of the principal organizatiors, both northern and southern. We stated that, in the nor h, there were Churches in almost all the various bodies, *is there were individual members in the Churches, who dissented from these views, and who came out openly against the atrocities of slavery, and hesitated not to declare slavery a *sin* and slaveholding *sinful*. These, however, are exceptions, whose very existence only serves to establish the charges preferred against the great mass of professing Northern Christians. Our object in the present article is to take a cursory glance at the relation of slavery to the great Missionary organizations and Tract and Book Societies in the neighbouring Union, and to see whether they do not, both by what they do and by what they fail to do, strengthen the slave power, impede anti-slavery action, and seriously injure, not merely the cause of civil and religious freedom, but the cause of Christianity, with which these are identified. Before entering directly on this subject, we would advert for a moment to the case of the Baptist Church, whose position and views we have been accused of misrepresenting.

For the benefit of the friendly critic who called our attention to this subject, we produce an extract from an article which lately appeared in the *American Baptist*, and which we submit, bears out fully the general statements we advanced in our former article. The writer, after saying that the Baptists have no great ecclesiastical organization to which memorials on the subject may be addressed—that the Churches are nominally independent, and may occupy such a position in relation to slavery, as they severally will, adds :—

" There is, however, practically, no such thing as withdrawing church fellowship from slaveholders, and still remaining in the denomination. The Church that excludes slaveholders from its communion, to be consistent, must also exclude those who commune with slaveholders ; and this would be to exclude the great body of the Churches, in the North as well as in the South. The hope has been cherished that the Northern Churches under a conviction of the utterly anti-christian character of slavery, might separate themselves from the Southern Churches, among whom the abomination is practised. But the probability of such a separation seems less, to-day, than it did ten or twenty years ago. True, there has been, from motives of expediency, a separation of the missionary and other benevolent organizations in which the two sections were formerly combined ; but the bond of " denominational unity" remains unbroken. The ministers of each section are cordially received by the Churches of the other ; and the constant interchange as opportunities arise, between the slaveholding Baptists of the

South and the non-slaveholding Baptists of the North, of the customary tokens of friendly recognition, proves that slaveholding is regarded by both as not incompatible with Christian character. Indeed the separation of the former from the latter, in their organized benevolent movements, is not to be ascribed to any essential and irreconcilable opposition of views relative to slavery. While the Southern societies are avowedly pro-slavery, the Northern are not anti-slavery, but merely, as they profess, neutral. If they are not openly and directly for slavery, neither are they against it. They put no difference between the slaveholder and the non slaveholder, but welcome both on equal terms. They make no discrimination between robbery and righteous gain, but receive, when proffered for the purposes they have in view, the fruit of unrequited toil, or the price of blood, as readily as the legitimate earnings of honest labour. In fact, the entire question of slavery is a thing which they ignore, as foreign to the 'single object' to which the different organizations have severally restricted themselves. Accordingly we do not find, in the published proceedings of these Societies at their recent meetings, a single allusion to this gigantic evil, this chief sin of the American Churches, as well as of the American people, this grand moral question which is shaking the nation to its centre, and moving the civilized world. The American Baptist Missionary Union, the American Baptist Home Mission Society, the American Baptist Publication Society, the American and Foreign Bible Society, and the American Bible Union, whatever else they may say, have not one word to utter, in condemnation of a system which reduces more than three millions of the people of this nation to the condition of mere chattels, merchandize liable to be sold upon the shambles to the highest bidder, which abolishes among all these millions the institution of marriage, nullifies the authority and all the rights of the parental relation, and tears away from them the key of knowledge, by sternly prohibiting their education. They are zealous to remove the heathenism of foreign lands, but they have no reproof for the system which creates a lower type of heathenism at home. Nay, with one consent, they receive to their fraternal embrace, as brethren guilty of no wrong, the men who openly support and defend the evil system which inevitably produces these evil fruits. And yet, these Societies, which thus turn away from the cry of the poor and needy, and which thus join hands with the oppressor, are sustained by the Northern Baptist Churches."

We have before us abundant proof to show further, that not only cordiality of sentiment prevails between the Missionary Union and the Southern Baptist Board, but also essential agreement upon the slavery question between the leading and influential members of both. It will be remembered, too, by many of our readers, how the Rev. Dr. Anderson, President of the University of Rochester, in a speech made by him some time ago at Brantford, apologized for, if not defended slavery, on the Southern plea, that it is irremovable ; and said that we must be content to wait for the period when it shall be removed in the general course and tendency of things. In conformity with these sentiments are those of most of the leading Baptist ministers of the North. The late Dr. Cone, of New York, claimed the paternity of the celebrated compromise which was drawn up to appease the Southern Churches who were so highly exasperated with those Baptist Churches that had previously passed resolutions disfellowshipping slaveholders. How this compromise was received in the South will be seen by the following paragraph which appeared in the "Biblical Recorder" a Baptist paper of North Carolina, immediately after the close of the Convention which met in Baltimore in 1841. "Our meeting," says the "Recorder," was truly delightful ; the spirit of the Gospel prevailed and gave a tremendous shock to Abolitionists. Let us be thankful to God, and give him all the glory. And now, if we at the South, and they at the North, whose sympathies are with us, shall be mild, I am satisfied that Abolitionism will go down among the Baptists. All our principal men are sound to the core on this vexed question. The triennial Convention exhibited a noble specimen of moral grandeur. About two hundred and fifty men, from the various parts of our extended country, were engaged in a long and arduous session, under circumstances that tried the temper and put into requisition all the intellectual energy which they possessed. And all this upon a most exciting subject. And yet, self-possession, calmness, the Christian spirit, predominated throughout the whole scene.   *   *   *   *   *

"At the communion board on the Lord's day, the scene was overwhelming. In view of the Cross, the hundreds that participated were all one. No test other than our dear Lord's requirements was thought of. To God be all the glory."!!!

Turning now to the Missionary Societies, let us see what is the position of the American Board of Foreign Missions, in which the Congregationalists, New School Presbyterians, and the Dutch Reformed Churches co-operate. The report before us declares that the action of the Board at its meeting at Hartford in 1854, "placed it in a position on the subject of slavery that should satisfy every reasonable mind." But its action did not satisfy every reasonable mind. What was the action referred to? Simply this: It refused to be bound by a law of the Choctaws which forbade the Missionaries of the Board to teach the children in their Sunday Schools to read even the Word of God; and farther, the Board endorsed the letter of Mr. Treat, one of their Secretaries, who visited the Indian Missions in 1848. Now, whilst it must be admitted by all that in doing this, the Board made a most important step in advance of its former position, still, when we consider the character of Mr. Treat's letter, and the circumstances of the country at the time of the Hartford meeting, we do not think that very much cause of self-gratulation exists. It must be remembered that Mr. Treat's celebrated letter of the 22d of June, 1848, nowhere speaks of slavery as a sin to be dealt with as other sins, and as a sufficient bar to admitting slaveholders to the communion table. It is true, it is severe against the *system* of slavery, but very tolerant of the *practice*. "A system of slavery" it says, " is always and everywhere sinful." Farther—" we do not claim that either Christ or his Apostles expressly condemned this system (domestic slavery) in the New Testament;" although he elsewhere admits that it is at war with the rights of man, and opposed to the principles of the Gospel. Such doctrine, then, is not and cannot be satisfactory to the consciences of anti-slavery Chistians. It will not do for the Board, the most advanced member of which is only what is called anti-slavery—a very different thing, both in principle and practice, from being an Abolitionist, be it remembered—to tell us that we must be satisfied with their conduct, so long as " overt acts" of cruelty towards slaves are necessary to disqualify for church membership. But in forming an estimate of the value of the late action of the Board, it must be borne in mind that, at the time of the Hartford meeting, the anti-slavery senti- ment of the North was raised to the strongest pitch, in conse- quence of the action of the Legislature in the Kansas and Nebraska matters; the encroachment of the slave-power had begun to alarm the Northerners, and the members of the Board were wise enough to understand the signs of the times. "Outside pressure" was thus brought to bear upon them. The Rev. Dr. Beecher said, "if you fail to meet this issue, your influence is gone beyond the mountains. And you must do it now, or you will never have another chance." The Rev. D. Pomeroy, one of the Secretaries, said "h e felt that it might now be his duty to say that he believed that the feelings of the country are such that though this action (a reference of the whole subject to the Prudential Committee, for the purpose of giving a quietus) might har- monize us here, it will not satisfy the people at large." The practical result of this may be learned from a state- ment of one of the most distinguished members of the Board, who voted to endorse Mr. Treat's letter, and who, since that time, said to Mr. Tappan, of New York, " there will not I presume, be any change at the Indian Missions on the subject of slavery." The position of the Board then, as stated by authority, is, in substance, this :—" Slaveholding in itself is not sinful ; the abuses of the system are to be re- garded, and slaveholders are not to be excluded from the Church." At the meeting of the Board in Utica, held Sept., 1855, the subject was again up and was " finally" disposed of. The Rev. Geo. W. Wood of New York, went out during the last year on a visit of enquiry to the Choc- taw and Cherokee Mission Churches. He presented to the late meeting of the Board a lengthy report, embracing the result of his enquiries and consultations with the mission- aries and churches. The conclusions thus arrived at are embraced in a series of propositions, and were unanimous- ly adopted by the Board. The following is one of them :— " While, as in war, there can be no shedding of blood

without sin somewhere attached, and yet the individual
soldier may not be guilty of it ; so, while slavery is always
sinful, we cannot esteem every one who is legally a slaveholder a wrongdoer for sustaining the legal relation. When
it is made unavoidable by the laws of the State, the obligations of guardianship or the demands of humanity, it
is not to be deemed an offence against the rule of Christian
right. Yet, missionaries are careful to guard, and in
the proper way to warn others to guard, against unduly ex-
tending this plea of necessity or the good of the slave,
against making it a cover for the love and practice of
slavery, or a pretence for not using efforts that are lawful
and practicable to extinguish this evil."

The report further states that there are now 20 slaveholders in the Choctaw Mission Churches, and 17 slaveholders
in their Churches among the Cherokees. "This," says the
Free Presbyterian," is the conclusion of all the high-sound-
ing professions of anti-slavery zeal and principle put forth
in behalf of the American Board by its friends last year.
It takes its place alongside of all the slaveholding Churches
of the land. Its principles and practice are identical, on
this subject, with those of the New and Old School Presbyterians, Methodists North and South, Episcopalians, Baptists, &c. These sects all hold that the legal relation of
owner and owned between man and man is not sinful, and
all claim that their slaveholding members are sustaining
the relation for good and benevolent purposes. They all
freely condemn slavery " as a system," but stoutly deny
that those who practice and uphold the system are guilty,
provided they are duly attentive to prayer and preaching,
and forms of piety. And this is just the position into which
the American Board has quietly settled down. " Oh, most
lame and impotent conclusion !"

While trying to apologise for the Home Missionary Society (in which Congregationalists and New School Presbyterians co-operate,) the Report admits its complicity with
slavery. Slaveholders fellowship in its Mission Churches,
and slaveholding Churches are its beneficiaries ! !

The course of the American Tract Society is now so
universally known, as to require from us at the present
time but a few observations. Through our own columns

as well as by the publications of Mr. Linton and others, its pro-slavery tendencies and iniquitous pandering to the slave-power have been abundantly exposed in Canada. The short-comings and sins of this society, as well as of the Sunday School Union, are severely condemned in the Report, whose title will be found above. Every sin in the decalogue is unsparingly denounced in the publications of this society " except that particular form of sin which involves the violation of the entire code—the sin of subverting the family relation, reducing the image of God to a chattel, and robbing a man of himself." It refuses not merely to publish the writings of " modern fanatics " on the subject, but excludes the testimonies of such men as Hopkins, Edwards, Wesley, Jay, as well as those Christian poets, Cowper, Pollok, and Montgomery. But not only is it guilty of sins of omission, the society positively suppresses the sentiments of authors, and alters their phraseology, so as to soften or destroy the testimony originally intended to condemn " a system at war with every principle of humanity, and every dictate of the Gospel." Wherever the word "slavery" occurs, it is struck out, and "intemperance" or "dancing," or "novel-reading" or the "use of tobacco," is substituted in its stead, thus "testifying,"in effect for the last thirty years, as the New York *Independent* lately asserted, " that the institution of slavery, the buying and selling of human beings, and the profession of the slave trader, are less offensive to God, less contrary to the Gospel, less perilous to the souls of men, than the practice of dancing or novel-reading, or using of tobacco." The Rev. Dr. Bacon, shrewdly remarked in a late speech that—

" *Sheer cowardice*, keeps them from publishing on slavery. They are ready to publish against dancing and against smoking, for from this they have nothing to fear. Those who dance and smoke will not fight those who do not, or who condemn these practices. He asked if John the Baptist might not have died of old age if he had the Committee of the Tract Society to give him advice ? If the Tract Society were sitting as a coroner's jury over his headless trunk they would have to bring in a verdict of *felo de se*. The moral sense of Christian men at the South may be right, but they are afraid to have the Society speak the truth. It is Atchison and Stringfellow, and the Devil and his angels, that make them fear ; and their timidity constrains the Society to keep silence. And whenever the Society are brought to publish a tract on the subject of slavery, even if it be a few pages from Simmon's Scriptural Manual, the pure and simple language of the Bible alone, and put it in circulation, every colporteur, every agent in all the South, will be molested and driven out, so that as far as those States are concerned, this whole system will come to a stand still. The inauguration of a new policy would unquestionably arrest the action of the Society. But, after long and careful thought on the subject, he was convinced that the present policy debauches the conscience of the North and of the South, and had come to have the decided opinion that if there were no connection of Christian bodies at the North and South, Christianity would exert twice the power at the South that it now does."

It is worthy of remark, too, that it is only in reference to Slavery *in the United States* that the Tract Society is dumb ; thus proving how valueless and hypocritical is the plea set up for silence, viz : the *Catholic basis* on which the Society is founded. On this subject hear the Report :

" Whenever the books of the Society do allude to the existence of Slavery, it is as to a system unknown to the people of the United States, but existing somewhere as a phenomenon in other parts of the world. Thus in one of the Society's books, where a passing allusion is made to a state of servitude, a foot-note explains that in some countries of the *East*, men are bought and sold and held in bondage. In some of the tracts on Temperance, arguments and illustrations are drawn from the slave-trade as this exists in Brazil and in Africa. Thus in reply to the objection of the distiller that he cannot sacrifice his property, it is said · Suppose you were now in Brazil and the owner of a large establishment to fit out slave-holders with handcuffs for the coast of Africa, and could not change your business without considerable pecuniary sacrifice, would you make the sacrifice, or would you keep your fires and hammers going? And again : If a man lives only to make a descent on the peaceful abodes of Africa, and to tear away parents from their weeping children, and husbands from their wives and homes, where is the man that will deem this a moral business? Other men will prey on unoffending Africa, and bear human sinews across the ocean to be sold. Have you a right to it? (No. 305.) Once more, speaking of the duty of rescuing the drunkard, it is asked, what would you not do to pull a neighbor out of the water, or out of the fire or to deliver him from Algerine captivity? (No. 422.) It is only with reference to slavery in the *United States* that the Society holds its peace. This studious avoidance of the subject, where alone the candid discussion of it can be of any moment, is a sad evidence of that fatal spell which the great dragon of the South has cast over many good men of the land."

We might allude to the course of the American Bible Society and other similar institutions, but we forbear. More than sufficient has been adduced to prove the monstrously inconsistent conduct persevered in and gloried in, by the leading religious organizations in the United States. There are, we again repeat, a few minor organizations of an anti-slavery character, but, as has been remarked "they embrace only such as dissent from the popular and prevalent views upon this subject." Among these may be numbered the American Baptist Free Mission Society, the American Missionary Association, (composed chiefly of anti-slavery Congregationalists,) and the Missionary Societies of the Wesleyans, Free Presbyterians, and Free-Will Baptists, all comparatively small and feeble. Can the religion, then, propagated by American missionary associations be of a purer, holier stamp, than that which prevails amongst the individuals composing these societies? "if these, " it has been asked " embrace only such a qualified form of Christianity as has no rebuke for the slaveholder, they will not be likely to teach a purer form to the heathen—since, to do this, would be to condemn themselves." How truly, did the Rev. Dr. Perkins, a missionary of the Board, who has attained a position from which he can now fearlessly speak out, say in a late sermon : " American slavery is the crowning abomination of the nineteenth century ; it is, perhaps, the greatest of human obstacles to the progress of the Gospel—the responsibility of its continuance rests much, if not mainly, with the Northern portion of our country, and especially *with the Churches and their ministers.*"

Some of the practical deductions from the above, so far as Canada is concerned, are the following:—In the first place, the ministers and members of the different Churches should make themselves better acquainted with the true state of the Slavery question in the United States. Judging from certain proceedings at some of our recent religious anniversaries, it is plain that a vast amount of ignorance exists on the subject. Then, again, all should feel that they have a direct interest in this question, and should use the means they possess to bring it to a happy termination. No commercial advantages, no political or social relations, should be allowed to stifle honest convictions, or to make us dumb regarding what we honestly believe to be inherently sinful. All communications with religious bodies or missionary societies which would imply not merely complicity with Slavery, but even indifference, should be studiously avoided; every opportunity of testifying our abhorrence of the system and of reproving those who tamper with it, should be embraced. Our sympathy with the friends of freedom, as well as with the victims of tyranny, should be manifested, and all our influence—moral, social, political and religious— should be brought to bear upon the extinction of Slavery, whose blasting influences even physical nature feels. In fine, no respect for ecclesiastical prestige should interfere with our denunciation of those

> " Who preach and kidnap men!
> Give thanks, and rob God's own afflicted poor!
> Talk of Christ's glorious liberty. and then
> Bolt hard the captive's door !"

THIRD ARTICLE.

In the two preceding articles we have presented a cursory sketch of the wicked action of the leading religious denominations and of the various missionary Boards and organizations in the United States on the slavery question. Much more of a similar stamp might be advanced, all tending to prove that, if the Church as a whole, has not been avowedly on the side of the oppressor, it has been practically so. It has not taken that high decided ground on this subject, which its importance and magnitude demanded. Its teachings have been of the "lower law" character, and have tended most materially to retard the progress of true Christianity, and in not a few instances to make infidels of men who unhappily judged of religion only through the medium of its professors. The following extract cut from a late number of the *National Era*, published at Washington, serves to illustrate still more fully the idea which we desire to impress on the minds of our readers. In an article headed " The Hon. Mr. Keitt and the Churches" the following sentences occur :—

"Mr. Calhoun, in his alarm speeches on the subject of slavery, was in the habit of referring, in ominous terms, to the agitation of that question in the great religious bodies, and its tendency to break up the connection between the Northern and Southern sections. Mr. Keitt, one of his disciples, is following in his footsteps. In a late speech at Spartansburg, S. C., intending to produce a weighty impression on his hearers, he announced that the Episcopal and Presbyterian Churches were in a state of great agitation on the subject of slavery, were on the eve of disunion, and that disunion was inevitable. The pious men of the South were scandalized at this, and the Rev. Mr. Baird stepped forth to defend the Presbyterian Church, and vouch for its pro-slavery orthodoxy. The bare idea that any respectable portion of its membership should be opposed to a system which invests one man with full power to make another man work for him without wages, to deny him education, and sell him like a brute, was not to be tolerated. The reverend gentleman vindicated his brethren of the North against the foul libel. This stirred up the Episcopal brethren, one of whom, the editor of the *Ashville* (N. C.) *Spectator*, addressed a letter to the Hon. Mr. Buxton, pastor of the Episcopal Church in that place. Mr. Buxton rejoices to inform the public that the community to which he belongs has really no history to present of its connection with slavery, 'for the subject has never once been named for discussion, or in any way,' in the General Convention of the Church. Perhaps, he says, it would be asserting too much to say " that there are not to be found private members of the Episcopal church at the North who hold extremely erroneous sentiments or are even fanatically influenced on the subject of slavery ; but such persons, it is well known, could not for a moment gain a hearing upon the floor of any Diocesan Convention in the land, not to say our General Convention.' As a fine illustration ' of the spirit of our Church press,' he adds, " take the following paragraph concerning the recent Wheeler case, which I cut from a late number of the *Banner of the Cross*, published in Philadelphia" :—

' We know not why the *Friends' Review*, of this city, should be continued to be sent to us, with marked articles in relation to the notorious, or rather infamous, Passmore Williamson. It cannot be supposed that we can feel the least sympathy in his behalf, or do otherwise than heartily approve the firm course and righteous decision of Judge Kane, who will not fail, we hope, to maintain the majesty of the law in this and all similar cases'—*Banner*, Aug. 25.

The beautiful, Christian spirit displayed in this paragraph renders proper the assumption by this paper of the title, " *Banner of the Cross*"! The editor of the *Spectator* adds his testimony :—

" We take occasion here to say that during a residence North of some three years, we became acquainted with several Episcopal ministers, and with many laymen of that Church, with whom we were in the habit of freely conversing in reference to the question of slavery ; and of the whole number of our acquaintance, we did not converse with one who was not decidedly opposed to the Abolitionists."

" We hope Mr. Keitt will be entirely satisfied ; and we see not what better he can do than to commit the holy cause of slavery to churches so entirely without spot or blemish."

We have already stated, however, that in all the great bodies there are some Churches and many individual members who sympathize not with the action of the denomination to which they belong, and who give forth from time to time on the question of Slavery no uncertain sound. We have named some of these, and might add several others to the list. The Progressive Friends, at their yearly meeting held lately at Livonia, Michigan, carried very strong resolutions denunciatory of slavery, of which take the following as a specimen :—

"Resolved, That, as Friends of Human Progress, we regard the institution of slavery as a crime, not to be perpetuated, apologized for and defended, but to be immediately, unconditionally and for ever abolished."

Then again several Synods of the New School Presbyterians have taken action on this question ; such as the Onondaga (N. Y.) Synod, the Synod of Ohio and the Synod of Peoria, Illinios. All these and others have lately denounced Slavery as unscriptural and inhuman and protested against its extension and perpetuation.

Farther, the majority report of the Committee of the Methodist Conference, to which the subject of Slavery was referred at its last sitting in Urbana, was to the following effect as given in the *Western Christian Advocate*. It is but fair to add that it was adopted by an almost unanimous vote, after a full discussion ;

"The undersigned, constituting one-half of the committee to whom was referred the subject of slavery, beg respectfully to present the following preamble and resolutions for adoption by Conference :—

"Whereas, the General Rule on the subject of slavery expressly forbids the enslaving of human beings ; and whereas, the voluntary holding of human beings in slavery, without reference to their emancipation, is equal in moral turpitude to their purchase for the purpose of enslaving them ; and whereas, we deem it proper to express clearly and definitely our sentiments on this subject ; therefore,

1. "Resolved, That we recommend the ensuing General Conference so to alter the chapter on slavery that it shall read as follows :"

"*Question*, What shall be done for the extirpation of the evils of slavery ?"

"*Answer*. 1. We declare that we are as much as ever convinced of the great evil of slavery, as it is contrary to the law of nature, the law of God, and just human laws ; and inasmuch as our General Rule expressly forbids its *initiation* and *practice*, by buying or selling, and, by necessary implication, forbids, also, its perpetuation.

"*Therefore*, no person who shall buy, sell, receive, give away, or retain as a slave, any human being, for any other than merciful purposes to the enslaved, for the purpose of emancipating them, shall be eligible to the membership of the Methodist Episcopal Church.

"*Answer 2.* Such of our members as may at any time have slaves under their care shall be required to teach them, as far as it is in their power, to read the word of God; to encourage them to attend upon the public worship of God, and to instruct them in regard to the sacredness and inviolability of marriage, and the duties of the parental relation.

"2. Resolved, That the General Conference make such other changes in the chapter on slavery as will make it conform with the preceding declarations of principle."

In a previous article, we alluded to the fact that the application of the Classes of North Carolina, to become incorporated with the general Synod of the Reformed Dutch Church, was declined, many of the Ministers being opposed to a connection with slaveholders. It appears that as at present constituted, there are no Southern Churches in connection with the Synod, and the feeling appears to be that if North Carolina is admitted, now the door will be open to slavery agitation within the Reformed Dutch Church, which will result in rending it in twain, just as it has already rent the Methodist and Presbyterian denominations.

The Philadelphia Presbytery of the Reformed Presbyterians or Covenanters, amongst other equally strong resolutions passed the following at a late meeting:—

"1. Resolved, That the system of American slavery is, in its entire character, principles, claims and issues, at war with the law of God, and utterly subversive of the dearest and most precious and essential rights of man.

"2. Resolved, That to hold or claim any human being as property—and consequently liable to all its incidents—as a *thing* to be bought, sold, and used for the owner's benefit, as slaveholders do, is a sin of the blackest hue, and should be regarded as a crime to be punished by the Judges.

"3. Resolved, That slaveholding admits of no apology, and that those churches and ministers that give their countenance to this sin, by admitting slaveholders to membership, and by refusing to testify openly and constantly against their iniquity, are not only recreant to the benignant teachings and spirit of the Gospel and of its blessed Author, but also to the claims of our common humanity, and deserve the high condemnation of the friends of Christ, of the Scriptures, and of man."

We need scarcely say that amongst the Congregationalists and those Churches which are subject to the control of no ecclesiastical body, there are many Associations especially in the Eastern States which are thought sound on this great question, and are bearing aloft the banner of liberty and truth. Again, we might refer at greater length to those

Churches which felt compelled to secede from the old
Churches and form local independent Churches. In 1834,
a discussion arose in the Methodist Episcopal Church which
terminated in the withdrawal of certain members in 1842.
In May, 1843, the Wesleyan Methodist Church was regularly organized at Utica, N. Y. and since then they have
gained numerous accessions. They have several missionaries in Slave States and through their Missionary Society,
whose office is at Syracuse, they are doing a very important work.

The Free Presbyterians are a body who came out
a few years since both from the OLD and NEW Schools. "It
was organized with only eleven ministers and their Churches, and mainly with the view of obtaining relief to their consciences from the necessity imposed upon them of being in
fellowship and communion with that great crime upon the
life of the soul, American slavery. It now consists of four
Presbyteries, covering Pennsylvania and Ohio, and the
Western States. It proclaims a divorce, total and entire,
between the religion of Jesus Christ and slavery. It re-
quires its members, as a term of communion, to neither use,
manufacture nor sell intoxicating liquors as a beverage.
And it is opposed to all secret societies as inexpedient, un-
called for, and therefore wrong. This religious organization holds to the Calvinistic system of theology, and in form
of government is strictly Presbyterian, having abolished the
life-tenure of the office of ruling elderand made it elective-
by the people triennially—thus approximating the order of
the Church of Scotland in the days of its greatest purity. It
has a weekly religious paper called *The Free Presbyterian*,
conducted with marked ability, at Yellow Springs, Ohio,
by the Rev. Joseph Gordon. It has also an institution of
learning in the same State, which, although in its infancy,
promises to succeed." Amongst the leading Free Missions, we would mention the "American Missionary Association" which is sustained chiefly by Congregationalists,
Presbyterians, "Free Presbyterians," and to some extent
by Wesleyans and Methodists. It was formed at Albany,
in 1846, and embraces Foreign and Domestic missions, having missions in Africa, Jamaica, Siam, Sandwich Islands,
Canada, Southern and Western States, and many other

places. Its active agents such as Lewis Tappan, Esq., of New York, and the Rev. Messrs. Whipple and Jocelyn, are men of piety and untiring zeal in the cause of freedom.

There is also the " American Baptist Free Missionary Society and the Free-will Baptist Home and Foreign Missionary Societies " all of which are making converts to the truth, and labouring zealously to neutralize, if not destroy the baneful influences shed abroad over the country by the upas tree of slavery.

What then is our duty in relation to this great, this weighty matter? Unquestionably, in view of the sinfulness of slaveholding, as practised in the United States of America, and of the tremendous evils which result therefrom, it behoveth Christian men, both in their individual capacities, and associated together in ecclesiastical organizations, to withhold fellowship from such Churches and other ecclesiastical bodies as tolerate and practice slaveholding. The question is not whether we should declare in our opinion all slaveholders in all circumstances to be " wholly destitute of the spirit of Christ, and fit to be ranked only with the ungodly; but it is this, whether such slaveholders and the Churches or other ecclesiastical bodies tolerating them, have not taken such ground and placed themselves in such an attitude, that we ought out of regard to the honor of the Gospel and the religion which we profess, to withdraw fellowship from them, if we are in connection with them? Does not their connection with slaveholding constitute a sufficient ground for withdrawing from them those tokens of approbation and fellowship which are common among Christians who harmonize with each other?" We think it does, and therefore, we would call on religious men in Canada to consider the matter as indivi__als. We would urge upon the leaders in our Tract and Missionary Societies to ponder well their actions, whether indeed they may not even in a remote degree be by their silence on the question, encouraging sin and retarding the coming of that desirable era, when the entire Church of Christ in all lands shall shine forth in the beauties of holiness; and when slaveholding, with all its monstrosities shall be found, neither in the Church, nor anywhere on earth.

APPENDIX.

I.

A MINISTER FOR SALE.

" There is an advertisement in a Kentucky paper of one for sale. He was a slave to a man recently deceased. It is stated in the advertisement that he holds a license to preach. Churches in want of a Pastor will please take notice."—*Anti-Slavery Reporter*, (London, Eng.,) 1st August, 1855.

It is to be supposed that such a " chattel," as the above, will afford " a good spec," in Kentucky and other places in the Slave States, and is published in Canada, as one fact, however glaring, pitiful and degrading. The authority is indisputable, for the *Reporter* is published " under the sanction. of the British and Foreign Anti-Slavery Society," London, England,—our " Free and happy land." No publication of the A. Tract Society or of the A. S. S. Union, giving information to explain the matter of the slave question, or to awaken feelings on the subject of Slavery, is published by either ! and that in their own land where American slavery perpetrates such a sale.

That such a fact as this sale has a counterpart, is furnished in the *Reporter* of 1st Sept., 1855, for *there* is undoubted proof, by the Rev. B. F. Sedgewick, a Presiding Elder in Western Virginia, who states, (and he says too, in italics, " I speak of that which I do know, deny it who dare !") " that slavery has, for years and does at this moment, exist in the ministry of the Methodist E. Church. A presiding elder, during the late session of the Western Virginia Conference, told me there were three of its members (ministers) who were slaveholders ! " The Rev. D. R. McAnnaly, also states, (as in *Reporter*) "Slavery is not a bar to communion in the M. E. Church North, any more than in the church South. Here in Missouri, Arkansas, Kentucky and Virginia, a slaveholder is admitted into the Church North as freely as any one else," and further on, it is stated on the authority of the Rev. J. G. D. Pettijohn, " a highly esteemed member (Minister) of the North Indiana Conference," who says, alluding to those who believe that since the division of the M. E. Church into south and north," they are now entirely free from all connection with slavery and slaveholders, I will introduce them to a person, who is in good standing in our church, who, a few months since, sold a slave to a Southern slavedealer—the most despicable character on earth—and when this slave was delivered to his new master, they had to tie him hand and foot, and throw him upon a dray, and send him in this way to the steamboat that was to convey him south to the New Orleans slave market. And in the same city where the above instance occurred, there was for many days in that slave pen, or prison, a slave left for sale to the highest bidder, whoever he might be, either a St. Clair or Legree, all the same ; after a few days, this slave was purchased by one of his old neighbours, who was not willing to see him sold to the Southern slave-driver ; and this slave that was thus sold was not only the property of a Methodist, but also of a Methodist preacher ! I stood by, on one occasion, and saw a member of our church, and a *class-leader* at that, purchase a slave girl, the last and only child that a slave mother had left. I stood and looked upon that poor mother as she kneeled before this man ; I heard her say, as she sobbed bitterly, 'O, massa, please spare my child ! O, please spare my last earthly comfort !' And in this way she continued to pray ! It seemed to me almost enough to move a heart of stone ; but he soon turned scornfully away, saying he had not bought her to sell her again, and thus tore her child away, where in all human probability, they would never meet again in this world. And I might continue and enumerate many more similar cases that I could vouch for their truth, but the above is sufficient." And to do away with quibbling and cavilling, which abounds so much with objectors in Canada, as to the American Tract Society, and A. S. S. Union and U. Canada Tract Society, &c., these statements will be found also in the *Auburn Christian Advocate*, N. Y., with remarks, &c. The Wesleyan Methodist Church of Canada fraternises with and recognises the M. E. Church, north, sells and circulates its publication and demits ministers to its care. But other Canadian churches are also culpable. The Wesleyan body are not the only Siloamites !

Again, the fact is, (whoever disputes it, let them examine the correspondence in the *Independent*, of N. Y., and other papers) that a Colporteur or agent of the American Tract Society, or of the American S. S. Union, can travel safely unmolested through the slave States of Virginia, Kentucky, and Missouri, and distribute his books, &c., as such are acknowledged as of pro-slavery origin, but the licensed and regularly ordained minister of the Cross of Christ, if he travels, must be mute and silent, as to the " peculiar institution" of slavery, &c., and if he is not altogether so, and even however cautious, even his very dress, will excite that which will make a free man ashamed of his kind. So much for the sum of all villanies— (Wesley) ; and "man's inhumanity to man—(Burns) Nothing of Tragedy can be written, can be spoken, can be conceived, that equals the frightful reality of scenes daily and hourly acting in the United States, beneath the shadow of American law and the shadow of the Cross of Christ.—*H. B. Stowe.*

J. J. E. LINTON.

Stratford, C W, 27th Nov, 1855.

II.

AMERICAN TRACT SOCIETY—AMERICAN SUNDAY SCHOOL UNION.

In addition to the various instances of expungings of which the American Tract Society is, and has been notoriously guilty thereby justly entitling it to be accused of silence, hypocrisy, insincerity and falsity, the following additional proofs are offered :—

1. Rev. W. Jay's "Morning Exercises,"—see preface, p. 7.

2. Mammon, or Covetousness the sin of the Christian church, by Rev. John Harris,—see p. 78.

3. Atonement and Justification, by A. Fuller,—12 mo., pp. 396.

In reference to the last, (No 3) it may be stated, that the author was a Calvinist, but all his views on the point, are omitted, and " the volume is made up of extracts from all parts of his works, ingeniously framed into systematic chapters"—so says the *Presbyterian of the West*, as quoted and referred to in an article titled " Colportage," in the Ecclesiastical *Record* of the (Free) Presbyterian Church of Canada, published at Toronto, C. W., number for January, 1855.   As to the "Colportage" and the aims of the American Tract Society, see its publication—"Home Evangelisation," p.p. 171.

Religious Book and Tract Societies, of Canada, including *Bible* societies and various religious church denominations in Canada, which hold fellowship or connection with the American pro-slavery churches and societies are again warned to " TAKE HEED."   The Wesleyan Methodist Church of Canada, in its connection and fellowship with the pro-slavery M. E. Church (north) of the U. S. (some of whose class leaders, members and even ministers, buy, sell and hold slaves),—the (Free) Presbyterian Church of Canada in its circulation and colportage of and giving credence by its *Record*, to the publications of the noted pro-slavery Presbyterian church (O. S.) of the U. S., and "Board of Publication" at Philadelphia—the Regular Baptists of Canada in an especial manner,—and some of the Congregational Ministers of Canada, instanced by Rev. Henry Wilkes, D. D. of Montreal, (January, 1856, and S. T. Byrne of Whitby, C. W., (January, 1855), with the Congregational Union of Canada in its vacillating fellowship,—should all now say " LET US BEWARE."

If every educated Minister of religion in Canada were to peruse the Book,—"The Slavery Question, by John Lawrence," 3rd edition,—Dayton (Ohio) 1854, pp. 224,—THE GREAT SIN of the fellowship of the Canadian Churches referred to, would be too clearly seen, and a proper knowledge of the question of American Slavery obtained.   See also Tracts Nos. 1 & 15 of the American Reform Tract Society at Cincinnati (Ohio). The righteous course pursued by the " American Missionary Association," 48 Beckman Street, New York, should be a pattern to Canadian Churches and Religious Societies.

The American S. S. Union dare not publish anything against the sin and system of Slavery, and, therefore, the youth of America are not instructed in anything of that iniquity, by its operations or publications, besides the objections otherwise previously advertised—shall its sinful course be encouraged by Ministers of religion and Students in the British Province of Canada ?

The Religious Tract Society of London, England, can furnish from a pure source, every Sunday School Library, and every Book and Tract, which can well be desired for general colportage operations in disseminating a pure knowledge by man's authority, of Christianity. See catalogue of long eight folio pages, obtained at the U. C. Tract Society's Rooms, Toronto.

A want of sterling honesty, *with humility*, in religious Teachers and in their profession, does much mischief to enquiring and truthful minds— and in the world—and is a curse to Christianity and to the Cross of Jesus Christ.

JOHN J. E. LINTON.

Stratford, C. W., 17 March, 1856.

III.

RELIGIOUS PERIODICALS IN CANADA.

1. The *Church*, Church of England, Hamilton, C. W.
2. The *Echo*, do. Toronto.
3. The *Churchman's Friend*, do, Sandwich, C. W., lately begun.
4. *Presbyterian*, Church of Scotland, Montreal, C. E.
5. *Ecclesiastical Record*, Free Presbyterian, Toronto.
6. *United Presbyterian*, U. P. Church, Toronto.
7. *Christian Guardian*, Wesleyan Methodist, Toronto.
8. *Evangelical Witness*, Methodist New Connection, London, C. W.
9. *Canada Christian Advocate*, Methodist Episcopal Church of Canada, Hamilton.
10 *Canadian Independent*, Congregational Church, London, C. W.
11 *Christian Messenger*, Regular Baptists, Brantford, C. W.
12. *Gospel Tribune*, Baptist Union, (Free ?) Toronto.
13. *Montreal Witness*, general religious paper, Montreal, C. W.
14 *Le Semeur Canadien* (Protestant) Montreal.

IV.

RELIGIOUS SOCIETIES—CANADA EAST AND WEST.

1. French Canadian Missionary Society, Montreal.

2. Grand Ligne Mission, Canada East. (It fellowships with pro-slavery Baptist organizations in the United States.)

There are Tract Societies in Quebec, Montreal, Kingston, Toronto, Dundas, Hamilton, Niagara, and London. They have circulated and sold, and continue, the Books, Tracts, &c., of the American Tract Society, American Sunday School Union, and appear to favor unduly, the publications of these Societies which have been denounced as yielding to the Slave Power.

The *Bible* Society at Hamilton, and, as likely other Bible Societies in the frontier towns and cities, also appear to fellowship with pro-slavery organizations of the United States. This should not be, in a British Province, apart from the question of *the wrong* committed.

It is hoped that the time has arrived, in Canada, when all manner of *fellowship* with pro-slavery and quasi-slavery societies and churches in the United States, will be discountenanced by the ministers of religion, and any other in official religious positions in Canada. It is not so difficult, for such in Canada, to obtain information of these Societies in this wise, by the question,—" What books or tracts do you publish, circulate, or sell, by name and mark, against American Slavery" ?